THE
FIRST
Christmas
JUMPER

(and the Sheep Who Changed Everything)

First published 2018 by Walker Books Ltd
87 Vauxhall Walk, London SE11 5HJ

2 4 6 8 10 9 7 5 3 1

Text © 2018 by Ryan Tubridy
Illustrations © 2018 by Chris Judge

This book has been typeset in Tw Cen Mt and Berliner

Printed and bound in Great Britain by CPI Group (UK) Ltd, Croydon CR0 4YY

British Library Cataloguing in Publication Data:
a catalogue record for this book is available from the British Library

ISBN 978-1-4063-8873-2

www.walker.co.uk

MIX
Paper from
responsible sources
FSC® C020471
www.fsc.org

RYAN TUBRIDY

THE FIRST Christmas JUMPER

(and the Sheep Who Changed Everything)

illustrated by
CHRIS JUDGE

WALKER
BOOKS

For Ella and Julia,
my very own pet lambs ~ R.T.

For Hollypark BNS,
where I learned to love reading
and drawing ~ C.J.

CONTENTS

CHAPTER ONE

THE MULTICOLOURED SHEEP OF THE FAMILY

I'd like to tell you a curious story the likes of which you have never heard before.

This tale begins with a sheep. Not a red-nosed one, just a regular, run-of-the-mill, every day, nothing-to-see-here sheep. Regular, that is, except for one very important detail...

This sheep, named Hillary, was ... multicoloured.

Red

Yellow

Green

Blue

Indigo

Orange

Hillary was a splash of delicious colour in a field of creamy grey comrades that looked like balls of cotton wool with eyes.

At the beginning, when Hillary first arrived at young Farmer Jimmy's field, most of the sheep thought she was odd, goofy, strange, funny-bad-funny and just, well, way too *mad* looking for their patch of grass.

But, over time, they got to know Hillary and they got used to the flash of colour. To them, she soon became part of the flock, just another sheep on the farm. They could never have predicted what their woolly rainbowed friend would go on to do...

CHAPTER TWO

ALL SHEEPS AND SIZES

There's lots we could say about Hillary. It wasn't just her multicoloured wool that made her stand out. It was also the fact that she did, in fact, stand out … away up at the back of the field, in her favourite spot underneath a huge oak tree.

The thing about Hillary is that she loved to daydream, to be lost in her own thoughts.

And for her, it was all about the lists. She liked order and she was the most organized sheep this side of the fence. She made all kinds of lists...

Shopping lists
* Grass * Clover * Forbs
* Try some hay today?

To do lists
* Eat * Sleep * Eat
* Nap * Repeat

And lists of lists she's looking forward to making in the future
* Favourite ice cream cone toppings.
* Best sheep action movies (she loved *Dye Hard* the most).
* Most delicious Chinese take away for the field (the sheep always enjoyed a good chop suey).

The lists of lists went on and on.

Hillary just loved lists; they put some order on things and allowed her to dream about life beyond the field.

Despite looking the same, the field was populated with all sorts of sheep who each had their own unique things that made them distinctly them. There was:

Joe who never stopped talking. About ANYthing.

Margaret who loved to eat daisies.

Marian who loved hugs.

Sally who was serious but informed.

Mo who loved crows. He read somewhere that crows were amongst the smartest creatures in the animal kingdom, they could pick locks and pockets if they wanted to!

Mo

Donna who loved cake and secrets.

Donna

Liz

The Silence of the Lambs

Liz who loved reading. Anytime, anywhere.

And then there was ... Brian.

Brian, it had to be said, loved unending small bleat. And he loved to direct it at Hillary, interrupting (what everyone knew was) her favourite daydreaming and list-making time (twilight).

"How's the grass there, Hillary?"

"Much the same as yesterday Brian, and yourself?"

"Same ol', same ol'. Any plans for the weekend? Will ye be making more of your mad lists and what not?"

"I will."

"You're a gas woman. Or should I say, you're a grass woman! Ha ha ha."

"Maybe we should leave the comedy to the comedians, Brian," Hillary suggested, hoping he might leave her in peace. But Brian wasn't in a rush to go anywhere.

"I know, but I'm on a roll here. My jokes aren't that baaaaad. Like, for a sheep at least?"

With the usual roll of her eyes and the hint of a grin on her face, Hillary always made her excuses and wandered off to her patch in the field.

CHAPTER THREE

COUNTING SHEEP

In order to understand Hillary, we should really have a close look at her friends and those who knew her best. Her field was a bit like your classroom, or maybe your kitchen at dinnertime. It was busy, full of chatter and there were lots of comings and goings. The sheep in this field, it had to be said, had a good kind of life.

They were tended to by Farmer Jimmy, who owned the field. He was a kind man who loved his wife, Orla, and his beloved jelly babies. He was forever plucking them out of his pocket and popping them into his mouth before launching into a conversation ... mostly with himself.

He was often seen chewing and chatting about the latest tractor brochure that had landed on his doorstep. Farmer Jimmy LOVED tractors. He loved the shine of them, the way they smelled, the big, thick wheels and the way they rumbled along the field like a tank

24

going into battle. He would often regale the sheep with his knowledge of the tractor world, telling them that there were 16 million tractors all over the world and — get this! — the biggest tractors can have up to twelve tyres and each of these are the height of an adult human!

The sheep were intrigued and listened intently while munching grass. They learnt that tractors weren't as slow as people think. In fact, the fastest tractor made over 121 kilometres per hour.

Out of all the animals on the farm, Jimmy loved his woolly friends the most. In fact, it was Jimmy who gave the sheep their names as he seemed to know

their likes and dislikes simply by looking at them.

He was especially proud of Hillary as he had never owned a multicoloured sheep before. The fact that she was such a curious and unique creature added to his interest in and love of her.

A typical working day saw him start his morning by leaving the house after a hearty breakfast – kissing Orla on the top of her head as she sipped her coffee – packing a fresh bag of jelly babies into his wax jacket, jumping into his muddy green welly boots and making his way down to the field to visit the sheep. He would lean over the fence, do his roll call and chat away to them like they were people he might meet down in the local corner shop.

26

He was quite certain that he spotted a flash of recognition in the sheep's eyes whenever he approached. (He was right, sheep did in fact have the ability to recognize both fellow sheep and humans, too.) Farmer Jimmy also knew that sheep were much more intelligent than they were given credit for and that, with a field of vision of 300 degrees, they could see behind themselves without turning. So, in some ways, they had eyes on the back of their head and always knew when he was approaching.

Hide and seek, as you might imagine, was impossible for them.

And so, Farmer Jimmy got busy checking hooves and teeth and wool. Brian was never happy with all this poking and prodding and used to give some backchat which everyone pretended not to enjoy as much as they did.

Here would be a typical exchange with the farmer, and Brian answering:

"There are my woolly friends now!"

"Ten out of ten, Sherlock."

"Those fleeces are lookin' just grand now so they are."

"And sure, aren't you only lookin' fabulous for your age. Not like mutton dressed as one of our youngsters at all at all!"

"You are loving the grass today, sure it's as green and glossy as ever."

Hillary joined in the general bleating which put everyone in good form. She loved watching humans smile at them and saying things like, "Ah look at them, the poor things are starvin', listen to them."

But, of course, what Jimmy didn't realize is that they weren't hungry at all, the bleating was the flock roaring with laughter at humans who always think they know everything!

CHAPTER FOUR

EWE
WISH!

Now, about the lists. You know now that Hillary loved to make lists. But, Hillary actually had one *particular* list that she really loved to make ... and one particular day of the year that she loved to dream about... The one day of the year that mattered to her more than any other in the whole wide world.

1. Not her birthday.
(That made her feel old.)

2. Not Easter. (A vegan, she didn't like eggs.)

3. Not New Year's Day.
(Nobody organized anything properly.)

4. Not St Patrick's Day.
(Parades freaked her out.)

5. Not Halloween.
(She was sick of nuts.)

NONE OF THE ABOVE.

Hillary was over excited about the one day when everything felt a bit special. The day when sheep were kinder to each other and made a special effort in the field to make sure everyone was happy and safe.

Hillary loved ... CHRISTMAS.

She loved every single thing to do with that magnificent festivity.

Every day, alone on her patch, she would chew and think and chew and dream and chew and wish. She spent 364 days like this with all roads leading to that flash of magic, that twist of joy, that kernel of kindness we know as Christmas. Her favourite list, out of all her many lists, was reasons why she loved Christmas so much. It goes a little bit like this:

1. The smells.
(Pine needles, cinnamon and fresh silage.)

2. The food.

(Selection boxes
with different types of grass.)

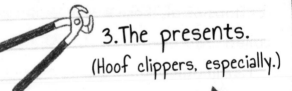

3. The presents.
(Hoof clippers, especially.)

4. The music.
("Fleece Navidad"
in particular.)

She loved the whole kit and caboodle. She dreamt of Santa needing to replace his reindeer with sheep and Hillary being selected as Commander-in-Sheep of that stupendous sleigh.

The other sheep often looked over and watched with amusement as Hillary gazed into space, imagining herself at the head of a flock of flying sheep, guiding Mr Claus through the sky and over the rooftops of all those odd human things called children...

Her imagination took her over oceans and rivers and mountains and countless millions of houses ... she imagined herself soaring, the wind in her wool, the smell of Christmas in the air—

"Howaya, Hillary."

She blinked into focus and remembered where she was. In a field. With ... Brian.

"Were you dreaming of Christmas again by any chance?" he said.

"You know right well I was, Brian. What else do I dream about?"

"I know but does it not get boring dreaming about tinsel and trees all the time?"

"Not if you love something enough Brian. I could dream of Santa and Rudolph and carols and cake all day long as it happens."

"Is that right? And tell me now, how *is* Santa? How's he getting on?" said Brian, teasing.

38

"Funny you say it, Brian. Santa was busy but I caught a glimpse of his lists. Both the naughty AND the nice ones and there in BIG BOLD writing was your name!"

"Is that right now. And tell me, which list was I on?"

"Ah now, that would be telling but I'll put it this way, Brian, you weren't exactly on the NICE list."

NICE
MAEVE
JOEY
DAVID
GEORGE
JUNO

NAUGHTY
(BRIAN THE SHEEP)

DONALD HUMP
PEARS MORGEN

Brian spluttered in response and bits of drool flecked with green came out of his mouth; his already bulging eyes nearly popped out of his head. For someone who thought that this was all a big joke, he was one worried sheep as he headed off to the far end of the field with his head down. He was really hoping for a fetching orange hessian jacket from Santa to see him through the cold winter months...

CHAPTER FIVE

TRUE COMPANIONSHEEP

You probably didn't know that sheep are very friendly and that they wag their tails when they're happy, just like dogs! And, Brian aside, Hillary did enjoy the other sheep and their baaaanter and she had one especially good pal.

But being Hillary, her best friend wasn't a sheep. No, her best pal was a starling named Didya.

"Didya" may sound like an odd name but it was Hillary's nickname for her feathered friend because of how he began every sentence he ever squawked with the same two words: "Did you?" Which always came out of his beak super fast as, "Didya?"

When she wasn't daydreaming, Hillary loved to listen to Didya's news bulletins. He was a curious bird and loved delivering the latest developments on the farm while bouncing along Hillary's back. Didya was the field's very own EweTube.

Through Didya, Hillary learnt all kinds of things:

"Didya hear that poor old Petula the Pig got stuck in her own trough?"

"And didya hear about the ducks staging a coup down by the pond? They refused to be put to bed anymore."

"Didya know that Santa is more popular than the Easter Bunny? Didya know that, Hillary? Didya?"

Didya, in return,
liked to listen to
Hillary muttering her
lists to herself, whilst sitting
atop her back, scratching it for
her and pruning her fleece.
Sometimes, he even added a
few things himself:

"Didya know
that my favourite
thing about
Christmas
is the bin?

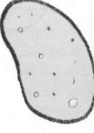

Didya ever see the
amount of delicious food
in there at Christmas
time? Oh now, the Brussels
sprouts and the carrots
and the potatoes and the parsnips!
Didya know that, Hillary? It's a birdy
banquet and my whole family gathers

around, squawking and
celebrating and asking
many, many questions.
Didya ever hear
the like?"

CHAPTER SIX

THE SHEEP OF THINGS TO COME

One day in November, Didya came flapping excitedly over to Hillary.

She had never seen him so full of beans.

"Didya hear the news, Hillary?"

"No, what news?"

"Didya not hear that Santa needs a jumper?"

"Santa? Seriously?"

49

"Didya not know that? The dogs in the street knew that. The cats in the cradle knew that. The fish in the sea—"

"OK, OK, I get it, Didya, but what else do you know? Tell me everything!"

"Didya know that he's searching the whole of Ireland for the best wool to make the first ever Christmas jumper?"

"NO way! But ... but he's hardly coming to *our* field is he?"

"Didya not hear the news, Hillary?"

Didya told Hillary about letters sent out to all the farms across Ireland from somewhere up the road (or thereabouts) called "The North Pole". She knew that Santa lived there and she knew that it was cold up

SANTA CLAUS
NORTH POLE

there, freezing even, but she also assumed he had a big red coat and that he'd be graaaaand (all sheep said this word in that way). But Didya said there was a rumour – Santa's sleigh rides were taking their toll, he needed to be warmer and he wanted the most perfect woolly jumper in the world...

Hillary knew that Irish sheep were the best in the world and that their fleeces made famous jumpers. She remembered postcards from proud cousins in Connemara telling tales of Aran sweaters and their reputation around the world.

Suddenly, it all made sense!

Hillary asked as many questions of Didya that she could think of. She was filled with a little exciting buzziness inside her...

Santa!

A woolly jumper!

Who would have thought?

Would Santa ever make it

to Farmer Jimmy's field?

CHAPTER SEVEN

ARE EWE READY FOR THIS?

We humans are mad for the weather. We LOVE talking about it whether it's too hot, too cold, too wet, too dry, it's always on the tip of our tongue whenever we meet another human. Sheep weren't as obsessed, but Hillary, it had to be said, was a big fan of November and December. November was always a cold month for humans and they loved to give out about that but for Hillary it was the best because she was at her warmest and her wool coat sparkled. With a light dew on her back and a strong winter morning sun in the sky, that rainbow fleece was a thing of beauty and although she was no show-off, Hillary knew she looked like a model who could rock the sheep-walks of Paris and Milan.

In fact, the other sheep knew it was November by simply looking at her walking around her patch of grass. (And by walking, they meant *strutting*.)

Hillary didn't notice them looking at her, she was too busy counting down the days to Christmas and planning what she might do on Christmas Day and what presents she might receive. If you listened very carefully you could hear her softly hum-bleating under her breath:

"**As shepherds watch** ... and then I'm going to decorate my fence with tinsel ... **their flocks** ... and then I'll try to sleep for at least two hours ... **by night** ... and then, when I wake up, there'll be all that stuff from Santa and then and then and then and then and then..."

On she went, standing underneath her favourite tree, words tumbling over each other and one idea catching up with the other plan and tripping on the next wish while skidding on a delicious dream. Hillary's head was so full she thought it might burst and then she worried there'd be demand for sheep brains in the local restaurant so she calmed down for eight seconds and started the whole cycle again...

Meanwhile...

Farmer Jimmy arrived at the field, and, on this day, he seemed extra excited. At first Hillary thought he had come to the field on his own to do his usual checks on the flock.

Normally, when he came at this time of the day, it was to do all the things farmers normally do when checking out their flock — patting them and commenting on their form or their teeth or their size.

But on this occasion, he wasn't alone and that's why all the woolly heads were tilted to one side out of curiosity. Hillary moved nearer to the action and on closer inspection she could see a man standing beside Farmer Jimmy. She was suddenly overwhelmed with a sense of familiarity, a feeling like being covered with a warm blanket...

To gather her wits, she made a list of
what she saw:

　　　* A very large man.
　Hot air balloon-shaped.

　　* Twill cotton shirt.
For the off-duty gentleman.

　　　* Shiny belt buckle, polished to
　　　　within an inch of its life.

　　　　* Black boots. Not expensiv
　　　　　yet impressive.

* Lots of hair.

* Rosy cheeks.
Like cherries.

Half-moon glasses.

* Old...
Over **100**?

Hillary's heart skipped a bleat...
Could it be...
No.
Never...
Maybe?
Possibly?

CHAPTER EIGHT

EVERY ONCE IN A WOOL...

☆

At this stage Farmer Jimmy was a wreck. He was popping jelly babies into his mouth like there was no tomorrow and talking at 121 kilometres a minute, much more than he usually did.

"It is such an honour to have you on my farm, I can't believe you're here. I mean, there were rumours and stories that you might be searching for a sheep but

sure, I presumed you'd be off to Killary
or Kissane... My nerves are gone to be
honest ... of all the sheep farms in all the
world and here you are! I love your work.
You're a legend, like, and
for you to be standing here
beside me is just ... actually,
it's a little overwhelming and
y'know there is something special
about this flock and I—"

"Now is not the time for worry,
my good fellow! Worry makes
a mockery of us all and achieves
very little apart from more worrying!
Let us not meet trouble halfway.
Time is flying, as I myself will
be in a few short weeks, and
a man in my position cannot be

cold. Goodness, no, I can't handle the cold despite what you might think. Goes straight into my bones."

"Of course, of course. Well, here they are and they're a grand bunch so they are, great craic and no bother at all. Beautiful white fleeces and luuuuuvely texture. Go in there now and put your hand through their coats and you'll know all about it. Take your pick, any one you like."

"Thank you kindly."

Santa wandered around the field, petting a sheep

here and there, bending down to take a closer look at Margaret and Joe's woolly coats. Under his breath and talking to himself, Santa considered the fact that there are over one billion sheep in the whole wide world and yet here he was … in a field in Ireland. There must be a reason for this, he thought. His instincts were always very good and he knew that, despite most of the world's sheep being in China, he would end up with an Irish one, a very special Irish sheep. Maybe not from this field, though.

He kept looking around but couldn't quite find the sheep he needed.

Eventually, he rose, shaking his head.

"They all look a bit the same," he said to Jimmy.

"Yeahbutsure, isn't that what you are looking for? Something white and ... woolly? As is tradition?"

"Indeed, indeed but I was hoping for something a little more ... interesting. I really wanted something *different* from all the others."

Young Farmer Jimmy knew just what to suggest.

CHAPTER NINE

IT HAD TO BE EWE

Hillary froze in mid-chew. Actually, it was a bit embarrassing as she had four human eyes and countless sheep eyes now all fixed on her and she didn't know whether she should spit out the soggy grass or just keep going.

She stared at the ground and just kept on chewing until she heard a mighty thud of boots approaching, matching the mighty thudding of her heart.

She looked up and met the gaze of the enormous man with the kindest eyes that she ever seen. She felt sheepbumps, as if she'd met someone famous, like one of The Bleatles, and for once, her mind went blank...

"I didn't even realize I was looking at a sheep!" exclaimed Santa, now crouching down in front of Hillary.

"I thought it was a mural or a toy of some sort! Goodness gracious, it's only when she blinked that I realized this beautiful creature belongs to this fabulous flock!"

Santa knelt down and looked directly into Hillary's eyes…

"You, my dear. It's you. I've looked all over Ireland for wool like no other and honestly, I thought I would have to wear a boring jumper but look at you... Oh, you're a clever one, I just know it and you, my woolly one, have made me the happiest man in the world. Allow me to introduce myself, I'm Mr Santa Claus. You might be familiar with my work. Now, let me think ... Hillary! Ah, that's it, I brought you an album last year by ... eh ... oh

yes, now I remember, it was that Irish band, Ewe 2. That's it!"

Hillary didn't know where to look.

She nearly fainted and really wanted to lie down but she was also overcome with excitement because SANTA CLAUS WAS STANDING IN FRONT OF HER and asking for her fleece!

HER fleece?

Of course he could have it.

CHAPTER TEN

THE MOTHERSHEEP

Farmer Jimmy opened the rusty gate as Hillary walked through her fellow flock to bleats of joy. All her friends got a little emotional as they made their way toward her. They knew how much this would mean to Hillary – Hillary who loved Christmas and loved Santa and who was always destined for something a bit special with that Benetton-bright coat of hers...

Joe handed her a few jelly babies he had collected from Farmer Jimmy to share on the journey. He reminded her that her sheeply ancestors were sacred to the Egyptians, so she was simply following in the footsteps of other important sheep and that she should hold her head high and represent her flock with dignity and pride. Hillary smiled and repeatedly reassured Joe that she had everything under control!

Margaret gave her a bunch of daisies. (Half-chewed, but it was a thoughtful gesture all the same.)

Marian gave her a "hug". It was kind of awkward with hooves.

Sally was worried. Sally was always worried. She worried that the rain was too wet or that the grass was too green or that sky was too high up. She meant well but she was extra worried as she sidled up beside Hillary, frowning. With a half-smile Sally wished her friend well but warned Hillary to be careful and not to talk to any strange elves.

Mo gave her a crow feather so she wouldn't forget him.

Donna made her a delicious grass cake that took her 37 minutes to make.

Liz wrote an intense but well intended
going away poem:

And now you have to go away,
I really don't know what to say.
Just don't forget your fellow sheep,
When at night you go to sleep.
And always know there is
    LOVE sealed,
In every sheep in our old field.

Brian refused to acknowledge what was happening and sulked by the fence, hooves firmly crossed, not looking at anyone. It didn't bother Hillary one bit. She was overwhelmed and shaking with excitement at the very idea of joining her hero at the North Pole.

With Farmer Jimmy and Santa close behind, Hillary trotted along the road back to the yard with her head held high and her fleece sparkling.

The trio made their way to the barn door which was pulled open, with great ceremony, by Farmer Jimmy to reveal the most extraordinary sight.

Hillary had heard stories from Didya, passed down from animals over the years — animals that had seen Santa and his reindeer from the tops of trees, from mountain peaks, from rooftops…

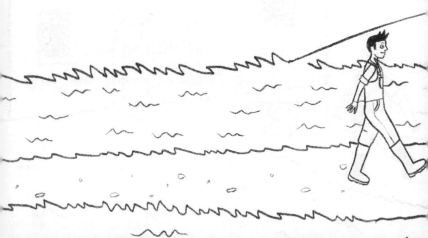

But nothing could have prepared her for

what she was looking at...

It was gorgeous — as impressive as one of Farmer Jimmy's finest tractors — but with elegant twists and curves.

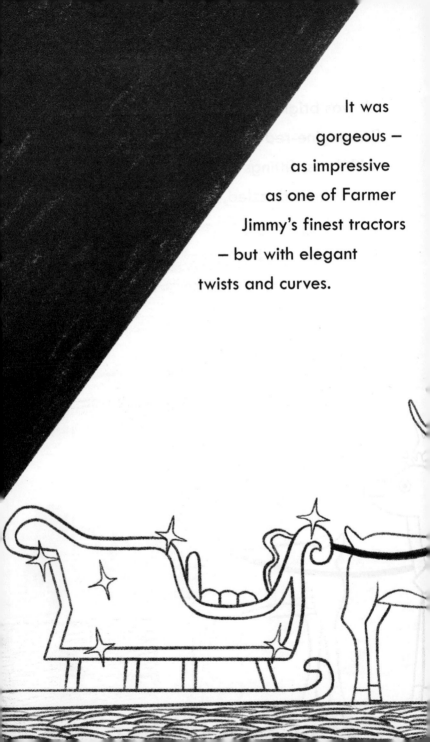

It was bright
fire-engine-red
with brass fittings
that dazzled,
even in the
dim light of
the barn.

The long stitched leather seat looked
buttery soft and after Hillary was helped
up onto it by Santa, she truly felt like she
was perched on a cloud.
Sitting in the sleigh,
Hillary noticed that there
were two burgundy velvet
pillows with gold tassels and
the letter "S"
on one and the
letter "H" for her one. A "H"?
How did Santa know...

On the back of the seat
in giant golden letters
were the words: *Ho Ho Ho*. And all along
the side of the sleigh, were thick, long,
black leather straps attached to the most
beautiful creatures she had ever seen.

Standing to attention and ready for their boss stood two of Santa's most famous reindeer that the world has known about for centuries – Rudolph and Dasher. They were taller and stronger than Hillary could have ever imagined – their antlers like elegant branches above their heads.

The fuel tank, it seemed, was chugging with hot chocolate as a sugary cocoa aroma filled the barn. Hillary saw Santa taking the key out of his pocket. And the key was a candy cane. This, of course, made great sense to Hillary who had dreamed of such things her entire life.

Just as the sleigh was preparing to leave the ground, Didya swooped into the barn and landed on Hillary's head, hysterical with excitement.

"Didya know this was going to happen, Hillary? Didya know that no sheep in the history of the world has ever been on this sleigh? Didya ever think you'd see the day? Didya?"

She shook her head, still in shock, still waiting for Brian to come along and wake her from a daydream.

After some discussion with Farmer Jimmy and Orla about his plans for Hillary, Santa put on his coat and hat and jumped up next to her, the sleigh shuddering under his weight. The reindeer started to clip-clop on the ground, their nostrils beginning to flare

in anticipation of the flight.

Santa shouted his thanks once more to Farmer Jimmy as the reindeer started to make their way out of the barn. Just as they did so, Hillary felt the whole contraption begin to rise off the ground and make its way into the skies above with an enormous *Whooooosh!*

The sleigh flew over the Farmer Jimmy's house and Hillary looked down to see her field, where her friends had all raised their hooves in salute.

She caught a glimpse of Didya flitting and flying from one sheep to another saying, "Didya hear about my pal Hillary? Didya hear she's making the world's first Christmas jumper, didya? And didya hear she's up there right now? With Santa Claus? Didya know that lads? Didya, didya?"

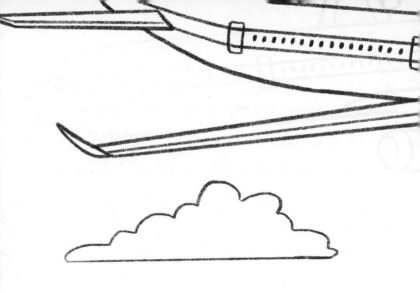

Santa shouted occasional words of encouragement to his reindeer as they galloped along on thin air, making progress through the skies.

He decided to treat Hillary to a bit of a detour so she could see all that the world had to offer beyond her field.

They flew over the Spire of Dublin, waving to Daniel O'Connell as they did so;

they skirted over London's Big
Ben; dazzled Hillary with the
glittering lights of the Eiffel Tower
and almost high-fived Lady
Liberty herself in New York City.
They flew over lakes populated
by hundreds of pink flamingos,
and they saw millions of red crabs
on Christmas Island. They even
passed the familiar sight of an
Aer Lingus plane.

Hillary looked into the airplane's window and saw a little boy peering back out at her with two eyes as big as plates. He started nudging his sleeping sister whilst staring gobsmacked at the scene outside. But just as his sister woke, the sleigh pulled ahead and she saw nothing.

She had to listen to the story of what her brother saw for the rest of her life!

Beyond this, Hillary was dazzled by an ocean of colours that danced and winked for miles beneath her.

She had heard of the Northern Lights from Didya but thought he was exaggerating and now there they were – a shimmering, swash of pale green.

And on and on and it got colder and colder and the reindeer shivered a little, tinkling the bells attached to their reins, but they didn't have to worry because minutes later, they landed with ease on

a strip of land that was whiter than the
whitest thing Hillary had ever seen.

And all that snow only made her seem
more colourful and shinier and brighter
than ever.

CHAPTER ELEVEN

JOLLY WOOL!

Santa jumped off the sleigh and took
Hillary by the hoof to help her off.
At first she thought they were alone but
as her eyes adjusted to the bright clear
whiteness all around her, she began to
see little houses and then the eyes of little
people, gathering all around the sleigh.

Hillary was looking at elves who had all come out to see the sheep that would change Santa's life forever. This was the sheep that would be responsible for the first Christmas jumper ever to exist.

The elves were as small as you'd expect them to be and their ears were as pointy as Hillary had heard they might be. They wore dungarees and striped hats with a tiny bell at the end of each one that gave

a little tinkle so that when they gathered around to have a look at their guest, the bells jingled in unison, giving off a beautiful sound.

"She is so beautiful," one oohed.

"She is so colourful, like the Christmas tree lights!" another aaahed.

"She is so fluffy, like a cloud!"

Hillary was exhausted. Her mind was whirring with a million different thoughts.

She was desperately trying to make lists in her mind of all the things that had happened already but she could hardly keep up with it all...

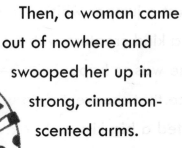

Then, a woman came out of nowhere and swooped her up in strong, cinnamon-scented arms.

"Ah yes, this is the very sheep we've been looking for, Nicholas. This is just the sheep to keep you toasty warm and stop those nasty colds you keep getting."

Running her soft, firm hands through Hillary's woolly coat, Mrs Claus smiled and knew that the sheep she held in her arms was not just a jumper waiting to happen but was a kind creature with a big heart.

She was so happy with her husband's choice that she went right up to him and planted a big kiss on Santa's pink cheek. Hillary's teeth stuck out as she grinned with delight.

CHAPTER TWELVE

FARE
THEE WOOL

Soon enough, Hillary was warming herself by a log fire and listening to a choir of Christmas elves singing Elvish Presley Christmas songs in perfect harmony — "Blewe Christmas" was Hillary's favourite. They had made her their special hot grassy chocolate, so sweet and so bitter — it was unlike anything Hillary's tastebuds had ever experienced.

Everyone wanted Hillary to be as relaxed and content as possible as her wool was shorn. After an hour, Hillary was ready for the shears. It was Mrs Claus who did the job and she handled Hillary in such a gentle, confident way that Hillary could have stayed there all night. As it happens, it only took a few minutes.

Bald, but blissfully happy, Hillary curled up on the couch with only the sound of a crackling fire to keep her company as she fell into a deep, deep sleep.

It took a few days for Santa's jumper to be ready. The elves in the JTU (Jumper Task Unit) gathered around five pictures hung on the fireplace, each one a possibility for the front of the first ever Christmas jumper. There was a penguin, a polar bear, a reindeer, a Christmas tree and giant bauble. There was much debate over which one should grace their boss's jumper.

In the end, they had to fold up the five pictures and put them in a bowl. Mrs Claus made her way over to the bowl and withdrew one picture which she unfolded slowly. Looking up, with a broad grin on her face, she announced to all present that it had been decided... The first ever Christmas jumper in the world would feature a certain red-nosed reindeer that they all knew and loved – Rudolph! There was general agreement that the right choice was made and that the terrific trio of Hillary, Rudolph and Santa made for a magical combination.

When Hillary's new best friend emerged from the kitchen in his new jumper, he looked at Hillary with a beaming smile. She nearly toppled over as she saw what her fleece had been transformed into – the very first, most beautiful, colourful and cuddly Christmas jumper she had ever seen.

Quick as a flash she conjured up another list, this time it was of the best things that happened in the previous twelve hours:

1. Being picked by Santa to make a jumper.

2. Making sheep, and human, history.

3. Being on THE actual sleigh that Santa drives to deliver presents.

4. Hot chocolate with Mrs Claus. (Total icon.)

5. The size of the boy's shocked eyes on the plane.

"Hillary, the reindeer are good to go. I'm extra warm and toasty in my new Christmas jumper and I'm going to put on my Santa coat and hat now. But I'll need a little company this Christmas Eve … it gets lonely on that sleigh, I can tell you! What do you think?"

Hillary didn't need any persuading. She simply replied with a grin on her face. She was the happiest, baldest sheep in the world.

CHAPTER THIRTEEN

IT WAS FUN WOOL IT LASTED...

After a helter-skelter trip around the condos, cottages, flats, houseboats and igloos of the world, Santa guided the sleigh gently over the west coast of Ireland, the Westerlies helping lift the sleigh along. Looking over the side of the sleigh, Hillary spotted the familiar sight of the Aran Islands and the Twelve Pins mountain range, all looking beautiful in

that magical Christmas early morning
light.

Within minutes, she spotted her field,
the huge oak tree she loved to stand
under and, behind it, the barn where her
adventure all began.

"Here we are, my dear. Home sweet home or rather, field sweet field in your case!" chuckled Santa to himself as the sleigh landed with a gentle thump. It was time for Hillary to say goodbye to her hero.

Helping her off the sleigh, Santa knelt down and hugged Hillary tightly. She tried her best to hug back but the hooves weren't great for the hugging so she snuggled in nice and close.

Hillary savoured her last moment with Santa, his candy floss beard, his warm cinnamon scent.

"I shall never forget you young Hillary and I shall always treasure this special jumper, one that I feel will be the envy of the world! Who wouldn't want a jumper with Rudolph on the front of it? And made of wool like yours? I've never been so warm and cosy on my sleigh. You are one in a billion."

Hillary was staring at Santa, wide-eyed and nodding. In fact, she was still nodding even after he had spoken, climbed back on the sleigh and lifted off the ground. She looked up just in time to see Santa waving. Lifting a hoof, she said goodbye into the sunrise sky until Santa, his sleigh and all the reindeer were little specks in the distance. She stared after them for some time, trying to hold onto the wonderful sparkly feeling in her tummy.

It was all so overwhelming that she didn't even notice Farmer Jimmy and Orla making their way toward her, Farmer Jimmy carefully plotting his path down the field amongst the dozing sheep, and Orla by his side, with an old lambswool throw wrapped around her like a shawl. Hillary almost burst with happiness to see their faces. They squeezed and hugged Hillary over and over.

"We're so proud of you," said Orla.

"Sure, we couldn't get any of the sheep or geese, or any of the animals, to settle long after you took off on your great adventure. Your friends have been looking up at the sky for you ever since you left. They've missed you like mad."

"We all have," said Orla. "And we know you'll be feeling a little nippy now without your wool, so ... I made this for you."

And from underneath her blanket, she pulled out a beautiful rainbow-coloured patchwork sheep's coat, with gold rope trim, to keep Hillary warm in the crisp winter frost.

It was a perfect, cosy fit. She was all wrapped up like a present.

"Merry Christmas, Hillary," they both
said.

Farmer Jimmy and Orla yawned, had a
stretch, had a handful of some jelly babies,
and gave Hillary one last squeeze before
heading back to the farm house. They
already had lots to do for the day ahead.

Christmas Day.

Hillary was almost too tired to think about it. Who would have thought? Hillary too tired to think about Christmas?

She made her way back to her familiar spot, looking fondly at all her friends who were still sound asleep, having tried to stay awake for hours in the hope of catching a glimpse of her with Santa. But well, as it turns out, not *everyone* was asleep...

There, under the huge oak tree, in her favourite place, was ...

Brian.

Hillary braced herself for some smart-ram greeting but she didn't get anything of the sort.

"I've ... missed you," he said, sheepishly.

Hillary couldn't believe her ears.

"Really?" she said quietly.

"Really."

"Thank you for saying so," said Hillary. "And I've got some good news for you."

Brian moved closer to Hillary. "You have?"

"I was somewhere very magical and I got a glimpse of the Naughty and Nice List ...

Brian, it's good news. Now go and check your spot in the field and you can see for yourself..."

Brian did something then, something that he'd never done before. He ... smiled. With genuine warmth and affection. It had to be said ... it looked a bit weird; his face wasn't used to moving that way. But Hillary smiled back. Maybe, just maybe, she and Brian were friends after all.

Brian skipped off to his own patch in the field and Hillary didn't have to see his face to know his joy as he put on his new jacket and sat down to read his brand new book, a maritime adventure (his favourite) — *Muttony on the Bounty*.

Just then, as Clarence the cockerel crowed in the morning up on the farm and Hillary's friends began to stir, tiny glittery snowflakes started to fall from the sky. Hillary looked up...

Snow.

Of course it was snow!

And with a gentle tip-tap, Hillary felt her good friend Didya take up his old position on her back.

"Didya hear the latest, Hillary? It's snowing. Didya meet the elves? Didya get any good pressies? Didya know how much I was missing you?"

EP-EWE-LOGUE

It was an extraordinary day in the life of a kind young sheep who dared to dream.

The fleece that made her different, helped to make her special and it was this that Santa spotted. It was only right that Santa wore the first ever Christmas jumper and it was agreed by all the sheep in the field and hopefully by you, reaching the end of this story, that Hillary was the worthiest wooliest sheep that changed everything.

BAA-HA-HA!

What does Farmer Jimmy say to Hillary while holding the gate open?

After ewe.

Where does Joe have his morning wash?

In the baaaaa-th tub.

What did Brian say when he stepped in a cow pat?

Ewe, that's gross!

How does Hillary greet her friends at Christmas?

Merry Christmas to Ewe!

What is Donna's favourite Christmas carol?

O Little Town of Bethlelamb

Where does Farmer Jimmy get his hair cut?

At the baa-baa shop!

What do you call Liz, who is always quiet?

A shhhhheep!

What does Sally read to keep up with current affairs?

The Wool Street Journal.

What did Brian want to be when he grew up?

A baaaaa-llerina.

Where can you find Hillary's field?

It's just pasture farmhouse, on the left.

What kind of car would Margaret love to drive?

A Lamb-orghini.

What does Hillary say when it's time for nap?

I'm going to hit the hay.

Brian: "Have you herd the latest?"
Hillary: *"What?"*
Brian: "Ryan Tubridy's readersheep are sick of sheep puns."
Hillary: *"I don't baaa-lieve you."*
Brian: "It's true. That sheep has sailed now."
Hillary: *"Hoof you spoken to?"*
Brian: "The pigs and the geese. But, shear up, I'm sure they'll come back into fashion."

What does Mo say when discussing his facts on crows?

I'm outstanding in my own field.

What did Joe say to Donna when she dropped a cake?

No ewes crying over spilled milk.

What did Ryan Tubridy's daughters say to him?

Manure making some awful sheep puns today.

What is Orla's favourite song?

"Everybody Herds" by R.A.M.

What ram-com does Marian love to watch?

Wool You Were Sleeping.

HILLARY'S FAVOURITE CHRISTMAS SONGS

O Come All Ewe Faithful

Winter Wonderlamb

A Winter's Tail

Mistletoe and Ovine

In The Bleat Midwinter

God Rest Ewe Merry Gentlemen

O Woolly Night

When A Lamb Is Born

Joy To The Wool

HILLARY'S
TASTY TREATS

Baaaaanana bread

Gingerbread ram

Swiss wool

Toasted baaaaagels

Prokniteroles

Crushed baaaaavocado

A Brief History
of the
Christmas Jumper

In the 20th century in Scandinavia and Iceland, where it is VERY cold (not quite as cold as in the North Pole, but pretty frosty!), heavy knitted jumpers were needed to keep people warm. But warm woolly, patterned jumpers really took off in Scandinavia with …
skiers! The ski slopes are fierce cold and the temperature can get down to -10°C (enough to make you want to wear THREE pairs of socks and two pairs of pants!). And so, they needed to be toasty warm as they flew down the mountainside. It was considered good for your health to wear the wooliest jumper possible as it would make you sweat which could prevent colds! (WHAT a jumper.)

Soon, the mountains and trees made it onto these woolly jumpers, and it wasn't long before patterns started getting more and more fancy! It soon became very fashionable to wear knitted jumpers!

By the 1960s, knitted clothes began to replace dresses and suits in Christmas ads, and warm woolly jumpers were soon associated with the festive season. And then, as clothes were able to be produced much more quickly, they became brighter and bolder and FULL of all kinds of crazy patterns ... as wild and wonderful as Hillary's rainbow-coloured wool!

Over the years, as Christmas has become bigger and bigger, the Christmas jumper has become an important piece of traditional festive clothing. I bet you have one or two yourself, or know someone who does?

Remember — Santa loves to see a good Christmas jumper! The sillier, the better!

Over the many years that he has presented *The Late Late Toy Show*, Ryan Tubridy has always worn all kinds of Christmas jumpers, including many hand knitted ones sent to him by fans. He even wore a striking black one back in 2011, decorated with … Rudolph's face! (A bit of inspiration, perhaps, for this book?)